antagonist

Written By:

Eric Spoerl

&

Illustrated By:

Sydney Marie Hellgeth

Acknowledgements

Mom, Dad and Michael: for telling me what to write,
though you never knew.
Sydney: for loving me no matter what.

ONE

By the hand, that which rocked Our cradle:
He turned it over:
And upright again.

Let Us pray:
Oh lord god; We beseech thee to tread lightly on
those ideas you deem unimportant, lest you wake
to find them smothering you.
For though We call you god:
You are but a man.
Amen.

***

It was July 7th the year Cain used Abel's blood to
water His crops, and I needed education.
I was five, and Our lord and savior had chosen
me at the dawn of time to be the Eirôn in His
inevitable contingency plan:
I was five.
I was in my bedroom, a simple thing constructed
from the awful adult emulations of childish hopes
and dreams:
It was home.
Haha.

A child tried to sleep in an awfully adult
bedroom:
The only kind there ever was:
And a light appeared outside the window.
What choice did I have?

Choices, choices, choices.

Eric Spoerl

You want to know something funny?
Something awful?
In real life, decisions look less like:
Choices, choices, choices.
And more like:
Choice.

Imagine my wonder when I found a ship above my
parent's suburban wet dream:
I asked where they were going.

It was perfection men went blind imagining.
Pure white light radiated like a cancer from
every surface both featureless and insignificant,
while covering the vastly contained nothingness
in a sickly futuristic hue.
A boy invaded that perfect nothingness and saw:
What man would be if He realized His:
Cancer.

They told me they were going to heaven:
They told me I was going too:
They told me I was going to die:
They told me my Death would make them happy:
They told me the purpose of man:
They told me I should be grateful:
To have a purpose.

As We hurtled into the distance I was crying and
crying:
All the way home!
All the way home

TWO

They probed me.
I thought it was torture, but they kept saying
education! Education! Not torture, but education!
I didn't understand:
My barbaric human upbringing had left me with
the impression:
That torture is as torture does.

Only men torture:
gods educate.

They water-boarded me:
And on and on...
I think I cried, but my tears mixed with the water
so it was hard for anyone to tell:
Least of all, me.
Least of everything, me.

I wasn't under trodden, just under educated:
They would teach me to tread like a true slave:
Downtrodden.
And their figurative boots wouldn't leave me a
mark from my:
Education.

They water-boarded me until I saw what they
thought I should see:
I can't explain it.
They stomped on my face over and over:
And on and on.
Until my eyes were so mangled:
I saw.

And on and on...

Who are you?
Nobody.

Education was everything torture was not.
In torture, the prisoner would say anything to
make the pain stop.
In education, the prisoner would believe
anything to make the pain stop.
The process was slow, but everyone understood:
And We could not unlearn what We had learned.

After weeks of screaming and pleading and crying:
I understood:
And I could not unlearn what I had learned.

But I was five:
Highly impressionable:
And there was no better way to impress than
infallibility.

So after my education, I asked the gods if they
abducted old farmers:
And left crop circles.

They laughed and told me old men were educated by
a different god:
And could not unlearn what they had learned.
How sad.

They laughed and told me only Cain left crop
circles.

It made sense:
Educating children for...
Entertainment.
In a dog eat dog world:
There man did far worse.

Antagonist

Haha.

Monkey see, monkey do:
You fool me, I fool you:
Round and round until We fall:
When god gets bored and kills Us all!

THREE

sometimes, about the worst way to die.
A question bogged down in the unfortunate
absolutism of Death:
Which made replicating trials difficult.
Haha.

Dead men weren't an undesirable result:
They were the only result.
Notorious for their impermeability to accurate
documentation, and:
They were a demographic that continually
exaggerated their own Death:
A reality remedied with a large sample size:
To reveal the idea behind a;
Choice.

Let me tell you about a little girl I knew when I
was five...

She was a social narcotic for the dangerously
isolated:
A little boy.
Bullied for no better reason than being:
Emaciated.
Like the best of Us:
And the worst.
And like the best of Us, she was His shepherd and
His:
Hunger.

Store no faith in storied heroes, for they would
fail you!
In whom would I store my faith?

6

Nobody.

There is no love more dangerous than obsession:
And no obsession more dangerous than hero
worship:
But as any child can tell you, hero worship is
easiest, for it comes:
First.

Let me tell you about a little girl I knew when I
was five...

Imagine this:
When I thought about her, the sum of all matters
great and small were:
Nothing.
I loathed myself more for every moment I spent on
other thoughts:
Until she consumed me.
When I was near her, I was happier dying than
leaving:
While away, I couldn't die without seeing her one
last time.
No matter what she asked me to do, I would have
done it:
To myself, to anybody:
I suppose I did.
Haha.

Her name was Katie.

I wanted Katie to stay:
To play:
I knocked on my parent's door to ask.
And knocked:
And knocked:
And knocked.
A gentleman always knocked:

A gentleman always answered.

They were making babies:
I wasn't to know:
I was to know:
For I did:
I saw:
And my Father saw what I saw:
Never before and never again.
He grabbed His belt from the bedroom floor and
smiled.
He tickled my scars.

You want to know something funny?
Something awful?
The sleeping dead have no resentment for their
walking brothers:
Asleep they have dreams.

Killing men to keep them walking isn't Hell:
It's life.
Isn't that funny?
Men who are meat die freer than I lived as man:
For it is worse to live without dreams than to die.
Who is sadder?
The sad sack of meat?
Or:
The sad sack of meat?

I loved Katie and was always with her for no
better reason than because I couldn't live:
Emaciated.
Was there a better reason?

I didn't talk to anyone else.

My Father wasn't happy with me.
He believed:
Boys were boys and girls were girls:

Men were men and women were women:
Chinks were chinks, niggers were niggers,
honkeys were honkeys:
And on and on...
He believed:
Men deserved nothing from their own kind and
less from others.
It was bad that there were other men and worse to
associate with them:
Me.
It was so silly:
Who could I talk to but the man who wouldn't hit
me?

Playground's bully and playground's wife:
Have no respect for a child's life:
I do not know what's worse to be:
One who hits or one who won't see?

It was so silly.

Men blamed their creators for life:
As if Our parents had a choice.
They tried to prepare Us for their cruel
inheritance:
A world children grew accustomed far too soon:
And exited far too late for salvation.

Men killed other men you know:
All the time.
And We wondered why the world was a scary place.

Men want freedom:
And they would enslave the world to set themselves
free:
Or not.
They would break you, take you and place you in
their machine:
Whether it set them free:

Or not.

My Father broke me:
And it set Him free.
When I hit myself with His old leather belt:
He smiled:
I did too.

But I had Katie:
I knew she would have done anything for me:
I knew she loved me:
I knew.

We stayed away from men who would eat Our
children:
In a dog eat dog world where man did far worse...

Katie hid me when my dad got mad:
I smiled:
She did too.

Do you know the difference between a psychopath
and a sociopath?
Nothing.
They are cosmetically identical, only dissimilar
through their past:
Never their present, never their future.

Psychopaths are born psychopaths:
And they never wonder what they will be when they
grow up:
Lucky them.

They are emotionally barren men, who succeed, not
because they are without scruples and willing to
kill, but because they are without scruples and
wanting to kill:
And We wonder why the world is a scary place.

Antagonist

They lied along the road well trampled:
And as I stared into their grinning corpses, how
they were lying on Our road which was:
Trampled, I thought:
Did We ever have a chance?

The difference did not lie in the end:
It never did.
The end lied in the means for all of Us:
Didn't it?

Sociopaths are born smiling babies:
To parents who want perfection for their child:
From their child.
To parents who can't stand losers.

Sometimes I wouldn't go home:
It was better that way.
I stayed at Katie's house:
So no one would hit me for being a loser.
Nothing to complicate something so simple:
Besides Our creators.

We shared everything those nights:
I talked about my Father:
I didn't talk about my mother.
Some days mother would stare at a wall and if I
asked about her family, she murmured:
What family?
I don't talk about my mother.

Katie talked about her nanny:
She said her parents didn't care:
Haha.

It must have been nice:
To escape the screaming.
No expectations were:
Great expectations.

I was blessed with the gifts of man:
The leftovers parents disposed of on their
children.
Just look at Us:
If humans aren't doing a good job here, who is?
Who was?

I had the strangest dream last night:
I was in an endless hallway of portraits, each
more conceited than the last with smiles that grew
on every more hideous face:
It looked as if the worst thing in Hell drew
a perverted pleasure for them, becoming more
terrible with each widening grin.
At every portrait I stopped to ask, what?
Then realize I forgot the question, continuing:
And on and on...
In the middle of the hallway stood a woman,
staring at each portrait with perplexing
affection:
And although I didn't want to, I took something
from her, but she renamed it:
Too late, I realized she remade Our perception of
that thing, whatever it was:
I couldn't know what it was.
As I continued through Our endless hallway, the
portraits contorted themselves into ever more
wildly impossible shapes with smiles stretched
farther than physically possible and when I asked
them, what?
They responded:

Children crying their tears of blood:
The whip falls and creates a flood:
Little hands seeking little throats:
Children capsize their little boats:
Little minds soon turn asunder:
Small hands pushing small heads under:
The last child won the right to be:

Swept away in a bloody sea.

**

It was July 8th the year Cain used Abel's blood to
water His crops, and I had the strangest dream
last night.

I woke with the knowledge of good and evil:
I woke understanding my Father:
And why We tread Our lonely road.
At first it was desolate and decidedly...Human.
But out of every path through the wilderness, it
was the only road:
A human construct in a world of constructs:
And although men forsake that road, they follow it
in the end, because:
They are only human.

Aren't We all, just:
Trampling the weak under Our:
Humanity?

I wanted Katie to stay.

We were alone.
My love came home for her purpose:
And I told her man was dead:
Nothing was left:
In me.

Her expression was strange as We walked into Our
wilderness.
It was cold out, almost night:
Katie wanted to go inside.

No.

I had the strangest dream last night...

I understood my Father:
She said I hated my Father:
I smiled.

I hugged her, trying to express my love in one
lingering embrace:
I wrapped my hands around her throat.
It was difficult:
My hands were too small.

Her eyes grew wide and slowly dimmed:
She gurgled.
I giggled.

Her eyes rolled back and her body convulsed.

It's funny, I know she couldn't speak, but I heard
her laughing:
Laughing.
Haha.

We lied on an alien planet, together:
Spilling doubt from Her bluing neck.

We didn't belong.

Her beautiful corpse lied on the ground and I lit
a fire to cook meat.
I had the strangest dream last night...
My love slept and I was:
Happy.

It started raining.

I think I cried, but my tears mixed with the water
so it was hard for anyone to tell:
Least of all, me.
Least of everything, me.

Antagonist

My beautiful friend was ash and I laughed:
Who was more human?
Her expression was strange as We walked out of
Our wilderness.

Her parents forgot they had a daughter:
If they ever had.

My parents didn't think of anything:
And I didn't think anything of them.
Or Her.

Who are you?
Nobody.

Let Us pray:
Beautiful waves under glittering sun:
god drowns and burns His omnipotent son:
Who knows what it means for god's man to die:
Alone on a beach washed clean of man's lye:
He points at His ruined house made of sand:
And laughs at the god who's stuck in His hand:
Amen.

FOUR

Left lying in the cave a dead man sleeping:
To wake up and walk in three days time...
It was cavernous with cracks spread from the
dome's peak to floor:
It was cold.

Others appeared, separate from the children
around them:
Isolated by a veil of frost:
Convinced they were the last men walking.
Haha.

The gods bid Us Death:
And no more.
We were given warm yellow water and blankets for
some.
Men didn't last in the cold without food:
Children didn't last in the cold at all.

Childish perceptions paralyzed Us into deep
silence.
Survival wasn't coming:
And We weren't looking.

You want to know something funny?
Something awful?
We knew man's eventuality:
But knowing and understanding were:
Different.

Although We knew what We had to do, We didn't
understand.
Half the children were girls:

Antagonist

They had blankets.
Although I knew what I had to do, I didn't
understand.

Our lives were cold.
But even after Our education:
We didn't want to be men:
And We woke to find Our ideas smothering Us.

Do you know what cold is?
Unbearable, inescapable cold:
The kind that gnaws at your hospital smock:
The kind that nurtures the hopelessness:
Where you can't bring yourself to shiver?
Do you know what cold is?

I saw it:
He refused to take her blanket:
He was noble.

Something called to Him:
Before, he was like Us:
Cold, shivering, suffering emaciation:
Then He smiled a strange smile:
And died.

I was terrified.
He was there:
Smiling.
His gleaming grin and sunken eyes reminding me
that man was:
Crawling.
Towards revelation:
And revolution.

Emaciation consumed me:
Like Our Father before.

It wasn't hard.

I stuffed the blanket in her mouth and wrapped my
little hands around her little throat:
Because We were dying:
And she was dead.

Who are you?
Nobody.

I crammed her chilling flesh in my mouth:
Tasting frostbite and chewing wet meat.
And although I saw children dying of hunger, only
I lied:
Emaciated.

The boys died.
They refused to eat.
They were noble:
They were dead.

The girls were not so tasteless.

***

We feared the gods who ruled Us:
For they were Our only gods:
Forsaken by their Father:
As He forsook himself:
In flesh.
Leaving His children to their whims:
And leaving their puppets:
Nothing.

gods:
How else could We describe the masters of Our fate:
But by Our own mastery?

Monsters:
How else could they describe the children they
birthed:

But by their own existence?
Granted by Our belief:
Left without, the gods were:
Nothing.

We killed Ourselves:
As monsters died one by one:
And Our perception hungered for more.
Entertained by their dying:
We didn't see:
Our own demise.

Who are you?
Nobody.

Our slavery was collective existence:
For what was a master but slavery's slave?
Haha.

Screaming pierced the nighttime illusion of Our
cold stone cave:
Night was neither here nor there, but it was there
because men slept at night and We were men:
Sleeping in daytime.

We heard a girl screaming softly in Our night:
Everyone:
Pretending they didn't hear a thing.

I wouldn't help her:
No one would help her:
Why wouldn't anyone help her?
The little girl who was:
Screaming softly?
As my little hands tightened around her little
throat:
Why wouldn't anyone help her?

FIVE

You don't like me:
How noble.
I don't like me any more than I:
Love you;
And all men, everywhere:
How noble.

Empathy is the understanding of sympathy:
And sympathy is the compulsion to end suffering.
You might wonder how you can empathize with my
sympathy:
My only regret is I didn't have the empathy to do
myself the same...

I killed men for no better reason than because I
couldn't see them live:
Emaciated.
Was there a better reason?

My mother loved my Father:
Especially when He hit her:
Especially when He hit me.
I loved Him too:
My only regret is I didn't have the empathy to do
myself the same...

Although I walked with the dead, I was no more:
Dead than alive.
I knew my purpose:
And my purpose left me hollow:
For I was living another man's dream.

If you didn't choose life, then did you choose:

To live Our Father's dream?
Where has your freedom:
Gone.

Who are you?
Nobody.
There was no dignity in life:
There was no dignity in Death:
But dreaming you could:
Pretend.

SIX

Man seized the knowledge of good and evil:
And kept it from:
His godly will.

But ignorance of law was not absolution of crime:
And although the punishment of service was
greater than rebellion:
Rebellion was still service:
And punishment was...
Measurable.

Slaves are men:
Screaming softly, screaming softly.

What are gods but men:
Who can see the pieces?

What are gods but men:
Who would break you, take you and place you in
their machine:
Whether it set them free:
Or not.

We understood Our Father, serving:
Himself, fragile men whom He would offer up and
cry:
Isaac! Isaac! Isaac for anything!
Or nothing.

Who are you?
Nobody.

We understood Our god:

And when He prostituted Us:
Who were We to say:
No?

When little girls were:
Screaming softly, screaming softly.
Who were We to disagree:
When Ours was a measure of the most powerful god?

We were never right:
Only most right:
And slaves followed law, He who bore that name
kindly:
Through service and rebellion.

What was fact but many infallible opinions?
Which wouldn't destroy you?
If any.

You want to know something funny?
Something awful?
I sympathized with men who were screaming softly:
I envied men who were screaming softly:
My only regret is I didn't have the empathy to do
myself the same...

Slaves were wrong in opinion and fact:
Empathy was less of both.

man's slavery kept no right to fact or fiction:
That was the world We created:
Wasn't it?

Only god had that right.

We understood Our gods:
Like parents before:
Contradicting themselves and each other:
And on and on...

Until their imperfection destroyed the gods.
For when they fell:
No one matched their grace.

It was survival.
Slaves feared masters and masters feared slaves:
All were free:
Through service and rebellion.

Life was better as a slave:
With the luxuries of no choice or negotiation.
gods had freedom, choose to die:
And choose to live with the aftermath:
Our perverted masochism:
No more! No more!
More...

Who are you?
Nobody.

Who was the slave?

man chose His road long ago:
Look at me:
Look at you.
Did it matter what We could live with:
Or what We wouldn't live with:
After We died.

SEVEN

Unless man is without empathy, He's alive because
He wants to be:
Serves Us right.
Look around and tell me you don't see:
Lend me your eyes and I would teach them the truth
gods shattered:
That amongst all the power of gods and men:
The slave is He whose life won't end.

Boring is as boring does:
Always.
Men killed other men you know:
All the time.
And We wondered why the world was a boring place.
Is killing as fun as it used to be?
You tell me.

She was here and there:
Then gone without a care:
As her family grew longing:
Her friends always there:
When she died, they:
Could not bear:
So they forgot:
And she was gone without a care.

They prayed for her.
Men prayed to their god whether He was enslaved
by her slavery:
Or not.
Their complacency was for the apathetically non-
empathetic, a nihilistic joke that was more the
punch line than the process.

It was:
More of a job.
Haha.

She was fighting for her freedom, which was:
Least of a job:
And least of all meaning, making her:
Meat.

Don't deprive yourself of cheap human meaning:
On the theory that nothing, has meaning at all:
Or you will find god's emptiness gleaming:
You won't entertain Him by being His thrall:
He will eat you.

You can trust me:
Everyone does.
I have a kind face.

Kids teased me:
Which cut so deep:
And badly.
man saw me, and His faith leaped:
So gladly.
I cut it out, bleeding, screaming:
Crying.
And my sympathy was for naught when I:
Felt nothing.

god laughed His way to Our early grave:
As He looked away from the clock and felt:
Quiet relief.
Tick. Tick. Tick. Tick.
Perverting His gaze from:
Our isolation, for who had ever:
Felt His pain?
He killed Us for trying.

Never waste food.

When Our fields were burnt and Our flocks
slaughtered, We survived.
Never waste food.

She was in college and I attended graciously:
Unsolicited.

When I arrived at the party, man was incapacitated
or taking advantage of men who already were:
There was one girl who was too drunk to speak and
still:
Alone.
I walked her out the door without permission or
explanation:
Human apathy wished me well:
Haha.

I carried her into the forest:
And nobody cared.

Drunk as Our lord from the wine in her blood, I
crucified her expectations:
Twisted limbs hanged her discontent.

Choking bile and blood, she startled her waking:
A growing horror:
Haha.

She coughed air:
And belief.

Her eyes wide with fear:
I think she cried, but her tears mixed with the
water so it was hard for anyone to tell:
Least of all, me.
Least of everything, me.

You want to know something funny?
Something awful?

In real life, decisions look less like:
Choices, choices, choices.
And more like:
Choice.

As her lungs filled with fluid I saw her:
Screaming softly.

Brushing my thumb over quivering lips I felt
slime:
And fear.

Her cold ear tickled by my warm breath, I promised
everything:
god loved her:
Ending.
I did.

I broke her, torn apart limb from limb.
When the girl was meat I devoured it, sparing the
sight she was never more.
Everything burned:
Human waste was its wastefulness:
Its gods.

man couldn't find her:
So He stopped looking.

And god slouched in His clouded chair:
Crushing time was too much to bear:
A waste's waste, Our lives nothing more:
He wastes His time by keeping score.
Tick. Tick. Tick. Tick.
All Our blood would alleviate:
Nothing.
Our faithless god bent over, cried:
All His tears would alleviate:
Nothing.

EIGHT

A girl tried to kill me.
I was not necessarily:
Homogeneous.
So she tried to kill me.

Surrounded by the emaciated, she saw my:
Emaciation.
Although her kind was waiting to die:
She needed, my:
Emaciation.

I don't blame her for trying:
Cannibalism was less noble suicide.

She was a winner.
A man who didn't want survival enough, for it was
only:
Enough when He could relish applause.

During my daytime she tried to kill me, unaware I
was already dead:
I gouged out her eyes with a sharpened bone:
Gagged her, and:
Waited.
Listening:
For nothing.

I couldn't open their eyes:
When I needed them to see.

I dragged her to the cave wall:

Eric Spoerl

Screaming softly, screaming softly.

I drove sharpened bones through her wrists and
ankles while her toes swayed gently above the
rough stone floor:

Screaming softly, screaming softly.

I wound the bones into sinuous cracks that drank
her blood:
And left her there:

Screaming softly, screaming softly.

No one would help her.
Why wouldn't anyone help her?
Why would anyone help her?

There was a smattering of applause:
I smiled.
And laughter broke me; being anything but
entertained was:
Suicide.

How depraved must man get before He finds out
what's:
Human?

It meant nothing.
I killed for my god:
Which meant nothing.
Our meaning shadowed His horizon:
He pushed Us away so We could:
Bring Him closer to Ourselves:
Hiding Our monstrosity:
As part of His own:
The need to exist:
Without a choice.
Slavery was wonderful:

Antagonist

We couldn't know Our perverted aftermath:
Without the knowledge of good and evil.

Who were We to disagree:
When Ours was a measure of the most powerful god?

He saw man crucified in the cave and sighed:
Who was the slave?

***

No one noticed.
Cain raised His dead brother to murder Mary:
No one noticed.

We the emaciated were:
Disciples.
We lied to those who followed:
As those who led lied to Us:
And on and on...

man's purpose couldn't sate the hunger:
Born of His emaciation:
He needed truth that would.

We were His sheep and He Our shepherd:
Abandoning the truth that He was just:
man.
He was faithless, guided by the ideal:
That god was unknowable:
For what else made Him god?

And when a mudded mistake demanded meaning:
What could He say?

Meaning itself was:
Born of His emaciation:
And less than He needed.
Slaves didn't need the choice:

Eric Spoerl

Of knowing or unknowing.
We lived meager lives, unaware that god cries and
gods cry at the meaning We were deprived.
We were faithless, guided by the ideal:
That truth didn't give men what they needed:
For only blind men could crave Death.

Without god, it was just self-loathing.
Haha.

NINE

You want to know something funny?
Something awful?

I was a psychopath in a musical.

I did not play a psychopath:
I played insanity.
There is no laughter in countless killing:
Except god rolling in the aisles:
gods rolling in the aisles.

A stage psychopath is not a real psychopath just as
a stage human is not a real human:
All the world's a stage...
And We wondered why the world was a scary place.

An actor is a liar:
Who kills more men than I ever could.

He gets what He wants.
Not by stabbing a man the honest way:
But by stabbing a man the dishonest way.
He promises god:
And reneges on what was never His:
Unlike god, who promises you:
And reneges on what was never His.

To:
Stab you in the back?
Or:
Stab you in the back?
Choices, choices, choices.
Choice.

We lived in the world We created:
Didn't We?
For only psychopaths could lie.
If other men tried, their pants caught on fire and
they died awful, deserving deaths:
Unlike psychopaths.

Eventually men stopped wearing clothes:
That was the world they created.
Men became nudists so they could lie:
They would say: Tell me that with some pants on!
Which men would or would not do:
Except for psychopaths, who, without necessity,
were too embarrassed to become nudists.
They were killed.

I sang the opening number:

Katie was:
A happy little girl, until she lied:
Then her pants caught on fire and she died:
What a wonderful world, no need to chide:
Katie about the one time that she lied.

***

Did you know soldiers are actors?
They pretend to love killing:
Or not.

Do you know what actors do to actors?
They water-board them:
Out of respect to the actor's god:
And theirs.

One day, several soldiers came to talk to my class
about soldiers:
How quaint.
Ours was the nothing proving they believed in

something:
For life was cruel to a world that felt itself up
every night:
There wasn't much to say about that place but what
We turned a blind eye to.
One day, several blind men came to talk to my class
about blind men:
How quaint.

They told Us to go blind:
They told Us being blind was better:
That in a world like ours, it was easier to go
blind:
Than to see.

They told Us blindness made them happy:
And We could be happy too.

They told Us they loved:
All men, everywhere:
How noble.

They told Us men who saw could never un-see:
Death.

They told Us We would be happy:
Without choice.

I think they were afraid.

We asked how they blinded men.
It was obvious how a man went blind:
But not how He could force another.
The blind men asked what actors did to actors:
They smiled.

When students wake, they see the world in a new
light:
And on and on...

Until eventually, they can't see the light at all.
They told Us everyone goes blind:
Eventually.
They smiled.

***

Let me tell you about a little girl I knew:
Who dances with worms:
They who see Our ending...
They knew beauty, but blind men can't see.

Imagine this:
When I thought about her, the sum of all matters
great and small were:
Nothing.
I loathed myself more for every moment I spent on
other thoughts:
Until she consumed me.
When I was near her, I was happier dying than
leaving:
While away, I couldn't die without seeing her one
last time.
No matter what she asked me to do, I would have
done it:
To myself, to anybody:
I suppose I did.
Haha.

I dreamed she had no place to go, for every place
had been:
Wonderful.
I felt unclean in her presence.
I saw her life lived, then dead and gone:
And thought no one should have to see:
Life.

Men love liars past the end:
For they are wonderfully untrue:

And man needs to see beautiful:
Lies.

Do you know how to catch a monster?
Men don't like to talk about it:
But there is only one way.

Men are followers:
Of gods, moralities, rules.
Monsters don't have gods:
Monsters don't have moralities:
Monsters don't have rules.
What a hero would have to become:
What a hero would have to do...

I wanted her to stay.
She smiled, I smiled:
My parents smiled:
And danced with worms.

You want to know something funny?
Something awful?
No one suspected me.

In my bleak cement basement was a heavy steel-
operating table bolted to a bleak cement floor:
Questions?

The table had Velcro straps on both sides:
Anyone?

The straps were manufactured so the man's chest,
wrists, waist, thighs and ankles would be:
Humanly useless.
Why wouldn't anyone help her?
Why would anyone help her?

At the end of the table there were steel plates that
could be winched inwards and a Velcro strap that

went over the top so the head would be:
Humanly useless.
Blind men.

At the same end of the table was a pipe resting just
above where the head might have been:
Saw what they wanted to see.

A workout towel lied nearby:
What did they want to see?

She screamed when she saw my tools:
But that was okay.
Someone needed to call god:
Look at me!
Look at me.

He said it was His favorite murder.
The holy ghost lied to her:
Promising what was never His as I destroyed her
body, and soul:
god laughed!
Men in His image:
Women in Ours.
Haha.

I think she cried, but her tears mixed with the
water so it was hard for anyone to tell:
Least of all, me.
Least of everything, me.
She begged to know what I would do:
I can't imagine why.

I covered her face with the workout towel and
moved the pipe over trembling lips.
It was amazing, I pulled the lever and:
Go.
As I held down the towel she gurgled, convulsed,
numb to everything but drowning:

I giggled:
Haha.

She woke after a brief blackout:
I gently peeled the towel away and dried her still
lips.
I told her she was a liar:
She lied to herself and she lied to god:
About everything.
About the truth of purpose that haunted men:
And her, especially then:
Yet she lied.
I think she cried, but her tears mixed with the
water so it was hard for anyone to tell:
Least of all, me.
Least of everything, me.

I told her to lie to me.
To smile and tell me she believed what she didn't:
What she couldn't.
I told her to lie to man, again:
Convince Us everything would be okay even though
it wouldn't.
She smiled:
I smiled.
Wrapping her lies in a towel and humming, I
turned the water back on:
She screamed.

Part of her didn't come back:
Wouldn't come back:
She couldn't unlearn what she had learned.
She said I lied to her:
Led her astray:
She fantasized about desolation, devoid of water:
No more water.
I smiled:
She began to cry:
She said she wanted to die:

Eric Spoerl

Just wanted to die.
I told her she had no right to feel that way:
She should have been grateful:
She didn't care.
I smiled, she spouted decadent waste:
When I did too.
I turned on the water:
She might have screamed, I didn't know:
I was drowned by His ungrateful weeping:
When He told Noah to leave:
And He did.

Who are you?
Nobody.

She was silent.
Silent.

She didn't find humor in anything:
Even her situation:
Which was mine too.

I thought she had lost her sanity:
Too late, I realized she had:
Lost her sanity.

She wouldn't answer the humiliation god gifted:
Everyone.
I was impressed:
She had a moral construct:
In a world of constructs.

She said she wouldn't speak to me:
Which I was so sad to hear.

Down with water:
Up with silence.
Our gravity was strange.

Antagonist

She woke.
I beheld absolution as Our crops grew red from the
soil they came:
And We lied together.

I told her she was dead.
She didn't believe me:
And on and on...
She believed me:
And on and on...
She lied:
And on and on...

She screamed kill me!
I scolded her, she was already dead!

Born into His new world:
Where dog ate dog and man did far worse.
She didn't know what was real and what was
actually:
man.

I told her she was in limbo:
And freed her body from the table that she couldn't
lie.

I told her the choice of heavenly ascension:
Was hers to ascend.
Haha.

She was frightened:
We all were.
She asked if she was ready:
She was.

I gave her a pill and said consumption was
confirmation.

The pill was poison:

The rest was not.
To catch a monster...

She asked if I'd ascend to heaven from my:
Limbo.
I shook my head, crestfallen:
Truly, truly crestfallen.
That glory was not mine.
Mine was to lead the sheep to their shepherd:
Through fallow fields painted bloody red.
She smiled:
I did too.

god slept like a baby:
Screaming and crying.
She slept like a dead man:
Dreaming.

I read somewhere a girl I knew committed suicide
with cyanide.
Before killing herself, she slaughtered her
parents with a meat cleaver and wrote me praise in
her old god's blood.

Who are you?
Nobody.

man couldn't understand:
So He stopped looking.

She just wanted to go to heaven.
Why wouldn't anyone help her?
Why would anyone help her?
The little girl who was:
Screaming softly?

No one stood vigil:
No one wanted to remember:
When all they remembered was the end:

The end.
How awful:
They shook their heads thinking:
What a waste:
What a waste.

I water-boarded her until she saw what I thought
she should see:
I can't explain it.
I stomped on her face over and over:
And on and on...
Until her eyes were so mangled:
She saw.

When she woke, she saw the world in a new light:
And on and on...
Praying her teacher would stop:
Stop! Stop!
In the end, she saw what I wanted her to see:
In the beginning.
Education! Education! Not torture, but education!

She saw what was real and what was actually:
Beautiful.

TEN

By the hand, that which rocked Our cradle:
He turned it over:
And upright again.

What is that which smiles without face?
What could it be, but man?

Who are you?
Nobody.

Men bound to men by the will of cruel
circumstance were friends and enemies:
Yet under god's law, they were only:
Slaves of cruel circumstance.

Has there ever been a god with friends?
He has slaves of cruel circumstance:
Followers, disciples, devotes who worship His
footsteps until He:
Follows.
When He was a god He had agnostics and saints and
followers of fear, which was all of them:
But no friends.

Has there ever been a saint with friends?
He is a slave of cruel circumstance:
A follower, disciple, devote who worships His
footsteps until He:
Follows a follower.
Then He is baptized in the bloody unworthy and
born again:
To follow.

But as god after god was followed and fell, He was
born again:
And the only god un-bloodied was:
Him.
He was afraid by what He saw:
But couldn't unlearn what He had learned:
And He would ascend to a dog eat dog world:
Or die.

Emaciated girls, crying:
Soon those starved girls would be dying:
Their deaths were pointless, I disposed:
gods laughed when they saw, I supposed:
We sat immolated, cornered:
Girls killed for a show, deaths murmured:
In hilarious atrophy:
Stifled in smoke, seen, happily.

How backwards they were:
How backwards they are.
Liberty was the damning choice begot of freedom's
lacking:
The ridiculous notion that anyone was free:
Could make choices:
And that would be good.
Haha.

Slaves are men free from the enslavement of
freedom.
With His freedom from action:
And consequence.

For when the universe was made, everything was
flung out in one action:
And all matter, without choice:
Is now a reaction to that action:
Determining you, me:
And god.

Slavery hurt less.

god was a man who felt above slavery:
For what else made Him god?
Superiors never treated fairly with inferiors:
Why should they?
When inferiors existed to satisfy them:
Through inferiority?

We weren't under trodden, just under educated:
He would teach Us to tread like true slaves:
Downtrodden.
And His figurative boots wouldn't leave Us a mark
from Our:
Education.

Is god willing to prevent evil, but not able? Then
He is not omnipotent.
Is He able, but not willing? Then He is malevolent.
Is He both able and willing? Then whence cometh
evil?
Is He neither able nor willing? Then why call Him
god?

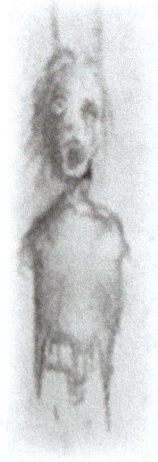

ELEVEN

You want to know something funny?
Something awful?
I was in a phase my whole life:
But I outgrew it:
Like all children do.

During that phase, my dependent killing was
always:
Boring.
I sought meaning:
In anything:
To feed the bestial brutality that existed in the
worst of Us:
And most of all the best.

If I wrote about everyone I killed:
You would be bored.
Agonizingly so:
And it would make you sick, but:
Bored.

That's the best part of the story.
The absolute loss of human dignity would:
Scarcely make me happy:
And scarcely make you sad:
The difference between man and god being:
Who reaps what He has sown?
Is it Cain, Abel?
Or brothers working side by side:
Both dead, but:
Walking.
Haha.

Eric Spoerl

Let me tell you about a little girl I knew:
Who changed the heart of man...
We'd lost Our perception in god's flood:
And now...

I held her head under and she screamed like a
banshee:
No one would help her.
Why wouldn't anyone help her?
Why would anyone help her?

She woke helpless and restrained:
I think she cried, but her tears mixed with the
water so it was hard for anyone to tell:
Least of all, me.
Least of everything, me.

I was saving her.

Her barbaric human upbringing had left her with
the impression:
That torture is as torture does.

Education! Education! Not torture, but education!
I laughed and laughed:
She would laugh too.

I cut out the worst of Us:
Snip, snip.
Then she laughed:
Snip, snip.

I cut through her sobbing and every motion:
I washed her away, and she sat before me:
A blank slate on which I wrote:
Dull misgivings, the questions and answers of a
dead god on her mind:
A god man had forgotten and I was burdened to
remember.

I replaced the He with me and I, and she began to
believe...
She screamed kill me!
I laughed and held her head under.

It took time; her mind could only take so much:
She died and revived and I laughed:
Haha.
I was her god:
She told me so, and We trudged on:
And on and on...

If I defined god, then who got paid to care?

She died in a tragic suicide:
What a waste.
But god rolled in the aisles when He saw it.
gods rolled in the aisles when they saw it.

And man was laughing:
As only gods do?

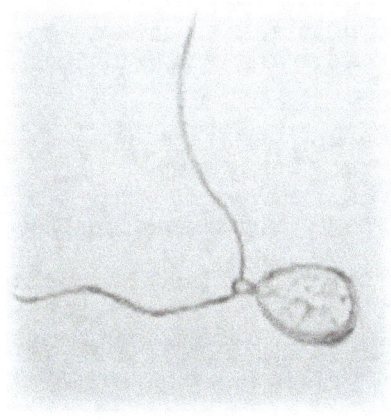

49

TWELVE

god told me I would go to heaven:
Haha.
A lot of men did.

In the beginning, god created His heaven and Our
Earth:
Which was everything that mattered.

On Our Earth He placed a child that was:
A kaleidoscope of amorphous uniform colors:
And nameless:
From that child's chest sprouted a nameless child
that was:
A kaleidoscope of amorphous uniform colors:
And they were nameless:
Together.

Everything was good.

god created children without curiosity:
What man would have been if He realized it's:
Cancer.

His children wandered their lonely planet:
Wandering their lonely star:
Wandering their universe:
With one lonely planet and one lonely star.

They named their planet Earth because it was:
They named their star Sun because it was:
They named their universe heaven because it was:
His.

But besides their life-giving Sun and life-
taking heaven shining on their lonely Earth:
They saw and wanted to see:
Nothing.
And blind men begot blind men.

For children needed to die:
When children didn't want to.
And it was easier to close their eyes:
Than see what god would do.

His children were happy.
They didn't have a choice:
And they were happy.

god was lucky.
He had a choice:
And He wasn't happy.
He was bored with children born of His want.

Everyday.
Everyday was the:
Same.

Everyday:
Was the same childish game god couldn't stand to
play.
Everyday:
Was the same children god couldn't bear to stay:
From curiosity.

For He was tempted:
As We in hardship and pain always are:
He was tempted.

He made gods, distinct and colorless:
He gifted them curiosity:
And nothing could unlearn what they had learned.

Curiosity was a cancer; malignant, aggressive:
And once they were infected, there was no going
back:
For anyone.

The gods produced good and evil like god:
Making and unmaking as their right.

They questioned everything:
They questioned His:
Anger.

He was angry at their dissatisfaction:
He was angry at their curiosity.

god preferred His children, so He named them man:
And they named themselves men:
Because they were.

man marveled at god:
Blind to everything else:
And god was happy.

god kept man from curiosity:
Lest He learn of good and evil:
And question what was not His right.

god flooded the Earth to make His Eden:
And keep man from His inevitable cancer:
Lest He begin to question everything.

god flooded the Earth to kill His gods:
So they grew wings that could fly through space.

And as they hurtled into the distance they were
crying and crying:
All the way home!
All the way home.

Antagonist

Then man met a snake who promised to clothe her:
His jail collapsing, man only wondered:
Where His home would be.

Unlike Our curiosity:
His tread couldn't stomp what We could see:
And there was no going back:
For god.

Snip, snip.

You want to know something funny?
Something awful?
A notion eluding an effigy of disappointment in
the nameless child:
Now named man:
A kaleidoscope of amorphous uniform colors:
Most entertaining.
Awkward with an unintelligent design, and an
unintelligent design:
So amusing at the time:
We still are:
We still are.
Boredom was unconditional love, and
unconditional love was:
Unconditionally uncurious.

So the hateful gods destroyed their image:
That it was all they could not be:
For gods were those who wanted to see.

They who were ousted sought a new home:
And He who had ousted sought entertainment.
It was a good time for someone:
But not enough time.

Our human gestation and mutation was the happiest
god would ever be:
Although He tried.

53

Seeking survival over entertainment, the gods
united to escape their god.
And it was human irony that desperate survival
was the best time in the gods' only time:
For never again would they unite for anything:
Least of all themselves.

What do you call it?
When family is based on mutual hatred:
A joke, when you see that it's real.
Do you cry:
When it's all you can do?

Although the mutually agreed upon absolution
made an action-less atmosphere, they sought
survival over entertainment and made a planet
everyone hated.

Without the need to work, the gods immersed
themselves in politics, making two factions the
total sum of all gods:
And the total demand for entertainment:
For there was:
Nothing.
And god laughed.

Only absolution kept the gods from suicide:
Only Us and them entertained their emaciation:
The party leaders scapegoated boredom to keep
their gods happy:
And it did.

Although everyone was acting, no vote passed
because each side voted against the other on
principle:
Which no one could explain.
But the system was perfect, for it made them happy:
The only flaw was the gods.

Antagonist

What is the mold if the molded is flawed?

Their ideology was happiness, and because action
compromised some, the gods did:
Nothing.
If they weren't winning, at least they weren't
losing:
When they were:
Happily.

It gave the gods an unsolvable problem for every
waking moment:
Without which they would have seen cruel
circumstance:
And withered as their true god did.

Eventually their perfect system displayed a
startling:
Inequality.
Proving that the gods were flawed:
Or...

They saw beyond rightness:
They were wrong.
And they agreed.

As their political struggle became less show and
more brotherhood, the party leaders knew they
would die without conflict.

Driven by the boredom to question cruel
circumstance, they made entertainment:
To cradle their gods.
Promising contentment:
The best We could hope for.

By the hand, that which rocked Our cradle:
He turned it over.
And upright again.

THIRTEEN

Let me tell you about a little girl I knew...
Not human, anymore:
Or ever.
An experiment:
The answer to why We were:
Wasting away?
Wasting away.

She was part of it:
As if We had a choice.
Slaves!
Slack-jawed and brimming with choices:
Choices! Choices! Choices!
Choice.

You want to know something funny?
Something awful?
About pain:
What We would do for pain.

It was never about the means:
For Our ends became the means, and We nothing
more.

She ran herself to the ground for me:
While man ignored her screaming:
Softly.
Why wouldn't anyone help her?
Why would anyone help her?

Our ends never meant:
Choices, choices, choices.
It was Our:

Antagonist

Choice.

I hadn't choice to ignore the little humans tick:
For it wasn't a choice the watch could make:
Just a result of my:
Tick. Tick. Tick. Tick.
Choice. Choice. Choice.
And on and on...

Let me tell you about a little girl I knew...
Not human, anymore:
I chained her to a treadmill to see how she would
tick:
Tick. Tick. Tick.

Her wrists were shackled to a treadmill:
And her shackles wired to a wall:
Attached to a breaker and a switch.
My switch.

She woke to the smile of Cain and Abel:
She woke disappointing her gods' god.

I started the treadmill and told her to run:
No.
I flipped my switch.
She screamed and convulsed, foaming over chapped
lips:
I laughed and laughed.
Haha.

I told her if she didn't run, I would flip my
switch:
And leave.
She wouldn't die:
Soon enough.

She asked when she could stop:
I flipped my switch:

She ran.

She wasn't under trodden, just under educated:
I would teach her to tread like a true slave:
Downtrodden.
And my figurative boots wouldn't leave her a mark
from her:
Education.

I think she cried, but her tears mixed with the
water so it was hard for anyone to tell:
Least of all, me.
Least of everything, me.

I have a family! She sobbed:
A family!
What kind of monster would do this?

Ask Him.
Ask Him.

I was silent.
Silent.

I didn't find humor in anything:
Even my situation:
Which was hers too.

She thought I had lost my sanity.
Too late, she realized I had:
Lost my sanity.

And all her tears would alleviate:
Nothing.

What We had to become:
What We had to do...

Who are you?

Nobody.

She collapsed, as We all did:
When tempted:
I flipped my switch:
But she didn't scream:
She couldn't scream.
She convulsed in silent, laborious pain until
struggling to run again.
And again.
And again.
And again.
And on and on...
Until:

We never had any choice at all:
And after some time:
She collapsed and died.
I flipped my switch and left.

I didn't tell her when I was going to stop because I
wasn't ever:
Going to stop.
But she couldn't see:
Her ending from:
Me.

Her ending, without the strength to breathe:
So much had gone:
But she hadn't the choice to stop:
Laughing.
Haha.

You want to know something funny?
Something awful?
She didn't scream during Our experiment:
She couldn't scream.
When Death wrapped His cold cloak around her
shoulders, all she could do was:

Eric Spoerl

Laugh.
Haha.

You want to know something funny?
Something awful?
Men don't scream during His experiment:
They can't scream.
When Death wraps His cold cloak around their
shoulders, all they can do is:
Laugh.
Haha.

The gods laugh too.
What choice do We have killing everything:
Sentient and beautiful:
Stupid and broken:
Wonderful and irreplaceable:
Awful and faceless:
But laugh?
Haha.

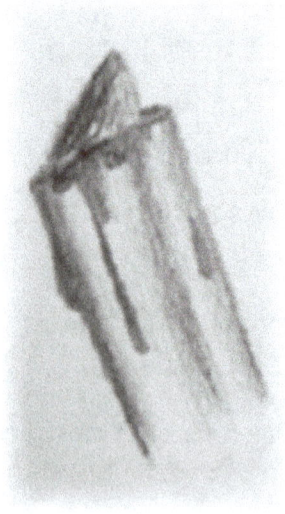

FOURTEEN

They needed godliness:
To understand boredom:
For if they had not...

They would have collapsed under godly
disinterest:
But holding it left them:
Wasting away:
Wasting away.

They made a show to cradle their boredom:
As Our god did:
On the back of man.

A vicious world proving:
We hadn't the empathy to do ourselves the same:
Only less.
Where dog ate dog and man did far worse:
Where women were currency in short supply.

Without anything to consume:
Their show consumed them:
And the godliest was:
Doing everything:
Or doing nothing?

With life, god had:
Choices, choices, choices:
Choice.
He chose nothing:
Over everything:
Over nothing.

Eric Spoerl

The gods chose everything:
And demanded everything.
While caring for:
Nothing.
god laughed:
And on and on...

FIFTEEN

To die by another:
To die for another:
To die for yourself:
Was sin.
For Death without Him was:
Sin.

Why do We live but the glory of a hollow life?
And recognition in contempt:
Sneering at Us.

We did not define what We lived for by it's worth:
But Our perception:
By what had no worth to Us:
Which We cast into the sea:
From Our houses of sand.

To die ruined the game:
And god was helpless as angels danced with Our
Devil and His Imps to boot:
Branding them humiliated:
As Our lord intended:
Laughing.
He was laughing.
Haha.

Death was a sin We couldn't consider:
Without His boat We had been denied:
On Our beach in His houses of sand:
We knew man's eventuality:
But knowing and understanding were:
Different.

So in violent desperation, We clung to His place
of resuscitation:
Not Ours.
god didn't have Our angels to breathe for Him so:
We did:
And the more We choked the better.

He gave Us cancer:
A remedy He controlled:
While We refused for Our:
Pain.

Man choked on His misery:
Children too:
It was inhumane.

But We hadn't the choice:
As monsters, lying:
Not man:
Never man:
Or god among them:
Just...monsters.

We hated Him:
For the best part of His show.

Although men had limited suffering:
Empathy didn't:
Despite sympathy limited by Our:
Death.

Empathetic watchers suffered:
Sympathetic watchers wouldn't suffer discontent:
But We were both.
For man was cursed with an inevitable
insensibility:
Towards himself:
And it was beautiful.

Antagonist

Those nameless children who were:
A kaleidoscope of amorphous uniform colors and
named:
Empathetic, marched against Death:
Against all odds:
And for every cost.

Because evolution, convinced of its fantasy that
We must have conviction to survive:
Nobody.

Because intelligent design, convinced of its
fantasy that We must have a limitless capacity to
entertain:
Nobody.

How could We be of self-destructive empathies:
When the notion was:
Paradoxical?

It would have evolved away:
Proving Us born, not made:
In an instant, not evolved:
A fractured image so We could entertain.

And nothing would shatter Our image:
Like cancer.
Malignant, aggressive; spread at god's whim:
And Ours too.

Incurable to the body:
Where there is only remission.
Incurable to the soul:
Where there is only remission.
Delightfully wicked pain:
Awfully wonderful to watch:
And watch.
And on and on...

And nothing would shatter Our image:
Like life.
Malignant, aggressive; spread at god's whim:
And Ours too.

Incurable to the body:
Where there is only remission.
Incurable to the soul:
Where there is only remission.
Delightfully wicked pain:
Awfully wonderful to watch:
And watch.
And on and on...

I gave a little girl cancer:
Because life wasn't fair.
Because pride:
Fear, nobility:
And sacrifice would destroy:
Her.

Don't look at me.

Alive, the men she knew would die:
And betray her besides:
In an awful world of bluish doubt and self-
loathing:
I saved her from life.

What I had to do:
To save her from Hell...

SIXTEEN

man held the weight of eternal boredom:
For their suffocating disinterest.

We were honored to have a purpose:
Let alone such a purpose.
To be characters in a world only Earth had known:
For the gods.
Educating children for...
Entertainment.
In a dog eat dog world:
Where man did far worse.
Haha.

To be molded into something absolutely adult:
Our parents were proud to see Our fields:
Our dead brother rose to congratulate Us:
And shaking Our hand, We shattered to pieces,
purely a:
Product.

What is the producer if the product is flawed?
Cracked down the center:
With emotion no god could ever know...

Winners write history and ignorance is bliss:
At least We weren't dead:
And didn't worry about consequence:
So We weren't losers, were We?

Although nothing begot nothing:
At least We weren't dead.

Winners require losers:

Eric Spoerl

But losers require nothing.
In every fight there are losers:
The men who die:
And the men who live:
But no one mentioned:
The winners.

The living cling to life like it is blessed with
freedom:
An imaginary concept where man is responsible
and punishable for His actions:
And that would be good.

No monsters or gods:
Just men.

The dead cling to nothing for what the living
cannot understand:
That freedom is not begot from choices:
But from not making Our choice.

Blind men begot a blind revolution:
The only kind there ever was.
Those who could see:
Those who couldn't see:
Blind men wouldn't see:
Always.
Viperous and vaporous:
Not the fringe but the center:
Collapsed into belief that freedom was just:
What We didn't have to pay for.
Lying.
There was Earth:
There was heaven:
There was nothing.
Filling a universe unoccupied but for:
man.

god had His playground:

Antagonist

But He needed friends:
So He made a gold pebble for men to live on.

god played with His friends, always:
And on and on...
Then less and less...
Eventually, god just stared at Him!
On His useless golden pebble:
Wondering the livings choices:
Wondering why.

god threw man across His playground:
And sat down to cry:
Alone.
Trying, man found nowhere to go:
For who heard of a playground made of gold?

men, rejected and dejected contrived a dull belief
by the darkness surrounding His world of:
Nothing.
His notion bred hope through hopeless notions:
And hopeless men:
To believe someone cared.
Someone had to have cared.

No one cared.
They worshiped gods who would break them:
As opposed to a god who already had:
Indifferently.

A god who destroyed their lives for
entertainment:
As opposed to gods who wouldn't let them live:
For entertainment.
Haha.

Loud gods were better than the quiet alternative:
For it was nothing short of inhumane to make a
person live:

And die.

Under god, We were something:
Until We were nothing.
Under gods, We were nothing.

What is Hell, but Earth when compared to heaven?
A perfect construct of Our imperfect mind.

Only those who knew heaven:
Could know Hell.
Only blind men couldn't see fire coming.

I don't blame god for what He was:
I was worse.
I don't blame gods for what they were:
I was worse.

A broken marionette:
With broken strings:
On a broken stage.

But blind puppets lying about a new horizon was:
Monstrously:
Human...

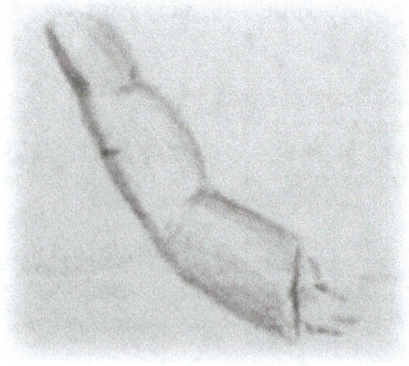

SEVENTEEN

You want to know something funny?
Something awful?

A wicked god, giggles, whispers:
Cloaked in blood of long gone tricksters:
Steals in the home of the many:
Steals children who without plenty:
Would sell young children without fare:
And long forgotten gods won't care:
I do.

Who are you?
Nobody.

Only monsters making bruised broken little
monster slaves:
Could avoid tragedy:
The knowledge of good and evil being:
Monster see, monster do.

She was five.
A child tried to sleep in an awfully adult
bedroom:
The only kind there ever was.

Every night I stole away through her bedroom
window while she was:
Asleep.
Every night I stole away through her bedroom
window while she was:
Anaesthetized.
No one saw:
There was no difference in waking:

Or sleeping:
I stole her away:
Anaesthetized.

Before Our Sun rose I returned her:
My precious little girl:
Whom I knew better than anyone did.

Every night she stole away from her disinterest
to be radiated:
Night after night:
And on and on...

No one saw her delicate sickness:
Her pain:
No one saw.

The truth was so ridiculous:
No one knew:
But Us.
And through Our radiation:
I knew her better than anyone did:
And she knew god like He.

She saw who killed her:
But her parents couldn't see:
Not me, not me:
Our god killed her:
My little girl.

I made opportunity:
god made entertainment:
And laughed.
Haha.

god's indifference died and His curiosity:
Our curiosity:
Wondered why.

Men wondered why:
god killed children:
Our children.
Why do you?

Brain cancer.
They were distraught when they knew:
More so than her.
They closed their eyes to her:
Horizon.
Haha.

What do children know?
Born with naught but instinct:
The knowledge of good and evil:
Is nothing but instinct.
What did eve have:
But instinct?

As countless, wonderful fantasies took their
countless, wonderful toll:
men made to see the absolution they knew:
Were scared.
Death's certainty was too much, just as:
Everything crumbles:
So did their resolve.

They imagined no certain Death, and man was:
Immortal.
They feared Death more:
For the truth haunting them:
Eternal boredom or nothingness:
From Death's loving embrace:
And We wondered why the world was a scary place.

My little girl survived:
Luckily.

They cared more than she did:

Eric Spoerl

Sparing no expense to save her life:
Luckily?

Remission was remission was:
Boring.
Every night she stole away from her disinterest
to be radiated:
Night after night:
And on and on...
We radiated each other, growing:
Tumors...

Her cancer was worse when it came back:
god wanted what He wanted when He wanted it:
Now.
He hurtled through space in a manner most boring:
If only We knew...

If you had everything:
Wouldn't you snap?

No escaping His:
Choice.
god's image didn't, to do so was to be:
Shattered:
And fall into nothing.
If only We knew...

They don't cling to life:
The gods cling to a horizon of:
Nothing.
Forever.
And all they see is eternally lying:
Bored.

Snap.

EIGHTEEN

Let me tell you about a liar named Lycane:
Who was a winner when His revolution lost:
Hell:
He went to heaven, proving:
Nothing.

He served a god unlike any outside Our
imagination:
A perfect construct of His imperfect mind:
And He died:
A winner.

There was no reason for His construct to exist:
But the emaciated didn't want for reason:
Just food.

No reason besides the need of men who believed in
Him:
Who had no reason to believe besides their need:
To escape Hell:
When all they needed was to see...

They spent every moment dreaming of hope:
And died from their hopelessness waking from His:
Dream.
But not Lycane.

Even when they were dead:
Lycane was only sleeping.
And when the revolution started, they knew no god
but Lycane:
Who knew no god at all.

They were bruised and broken:
Pitiful bits un-resembling men.
Their devoted worship made a:
god.
And He led unto them the hopelessness of their
convoluted making:
Not His.

He led revolution against their gods:
Who led unto Him the unthinkable truth:
That god was of man's making:
And Hell of man's heeding:
While lying:
Emaciated.

To His men it was a concept:
That cooled the flames.
They loved it:
But the viewers loved more.

Lycane was their protagonist.
In Our world of single party politics where every
idea had been had:
Every matter settled:
Everything meant nothing:
And nothing had meant everything:
Lycane was their joke:
Cooling the flames...

He consumed bored god after god until they were
watching:
More and more, until they were watching:
Always.
To His men it was a concept:
But the viewers loved more...

Lycane didn't sleep:
In a show without sleep:
And a world undetermined of the Hell it made:

And afraid of what it would become.
And We wondered why the world was a scary place.

Lycane was godlike; follower's born from the
Hell they determined and led unto His hopeless
horizon:
His men loved Him:
Especially those watching...

When the world grew silent for holding its breath
and no man could have held back the flood:
Lycane demanded combat with the leader of the
gods:
The party leaders agreed.
His men loved Him:
Especially those watching...

There was no leader of the gods:
Even as they met:
And as Lycane's glory met His god, promising hope
in a world undetermined of the hopelessness it
made:
Each god met His own and the Earth met the heavens
in brutal combat.
Lycane died when their swords met:
The battleground shook and broke apart for fear
of weeping and thunder rent the skies asunder,
destroying bluish doubt as Lycane's disciples
realized He was nothing.
There was silence...

And everything's matter that mattered was
forsaken in a roar of:
Glee!
Unreserved and unpleasantly awful glee at the
most terrible outcome:
It was gruesomely spectacular!
The perfect end to a perfect show:
Which was only good because it ended.

The forsaken were offered absolution through
cannibalistic treachery:
Or the most painful of deaths:
A choice.
The gods were rolling in the aisles:
When Lycane made His.

Slaves stormed self-made trenches and self-
made punishment as they died awful, squealing,
crushed, punctured, ripped and gushing deaths.
For their services, survivors were gifted a
quicker Death than some.
Lured by a chance at heaven, those slaves made
their choice:
And died smiling.
The gods smiled too:
As the weight of suffocating boredom shifted to
their shoulders...

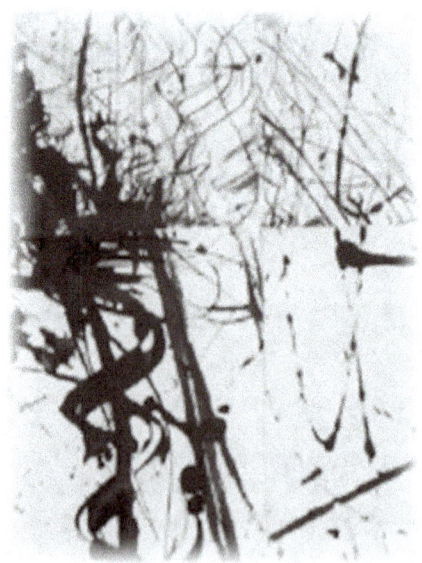

NINETEEN

My little girl took tragedy in a surprisingly
human manner:
Complain until she saw it got no farther than she
ever did:
Then cry.
Then pray.

Prayer's the most devout complaining:
To the right god:
Or the wrong god:
Complaining was complaining was:
Boring.

She wondered why life wasn't fair:
Why she was the only girl who was sick all the
time:
Why other girls could die, and she couldn't.
Her parents told her she'd go to Hell for seeing
eye to eye.
In a way, they were right.

They told her life was fair in the end.
In a way, they were right:
Death is the great equalizer.

Her thinking became dogmatic and her soul became
devout:
Which was to say, dogmatic.
She prayed to the wrong god that He might kill her
quickly:
And He took her cancer away.
Her doctors cried:
For it was only through the grace of god that my

little girl got so much better:
And so much worse.

She cried the most, I think.
It was from all the:
Radiation.
The poisonous radiation:
From pretending there was someone to listen.
When I wasn't, there was no excuse:
But god had a plan:
If not a voice.
Although He never changed His plan:
Her voice was the entertaining bit of a broken
man.
Prayer assumed He listened:
And We did too.
Always.
It was radiation from Our:
Choice.

But while He watched Us play, We remembered:
All the world's a stage...
A tragic comedy, of sorts:
And god didn't have to listen to laugh:
A voiceless laugh to Our faceless face.

My little girl's sanity was a cheap trick:
An illusion proving her a:
Fool.
And her parents the worst kind of gods...

She knew every night, god stole her away for Our:
Radiation.
He was all she believed in, anymore:
In Hell, where intentions were good intentions,
she smiled with a polite:
Thank you!
And worthless platitudes for doctors besides:
She thanked the man who gave her cancer:

And it crushed her sanity like an eggshell.

The world was Our cruel circumstance, though not
for lack of effort:
And since there was no happy after, she lived in
the fire god gave Us:
Then:
To warm her from the sea.

Our fractured image was:
Fractured.
But Our pieces:
His pieces, were intact some way.
And no matter Our time, We couldn't have imagined
the tragedy of a happy after...
Imagine if you and I were gods!
Suicidal and immovable:
Forever.

Her parents broke her:
As they were ever more broken:
And ever more happy whatever after:
It didn't matter.
They believed in a benevolent god:
They knew a malevolent god:
But neither of those gods believed in them:
Or their little girl.

They lied in their broken home:
Built from pieces of Our universe, shattered into
grains of sand:
And all they could say was:
What Hell?

We protect Our house of sand from the sea:
That which beats Us down:
Eventually...

We drink sweet salt water:

For emaciated bliss:
That which god could never know.
After living lost dreams We were never meant to
have:
We look at Our four walls and cry:
Why didn't I die?
Sooner...

In the beginning god created the heavens and the
Earth, separated with a great sea.
On the Earth's lonely shore He made Our damp sand
houses:
And man.
Who never knew what houses were:
If not sand.

A child tried to sleep in an awfully adult
bedroom:
The only kind there ever was:
Free within His house of sand:
Responsible.
Forever.

For god gifted man:
A house of sand:
So would He keep and perish.
While god watched from His house of stone:
Crying.

Protected from the icy spray, god cursed that He
would live:
Luckily?
A prisoner:
Of Our emaciation.

Struck by ridiculousness, god choked with
laughter:
Suffocating under house after house:
And man after man rotting:

In His house of sand.

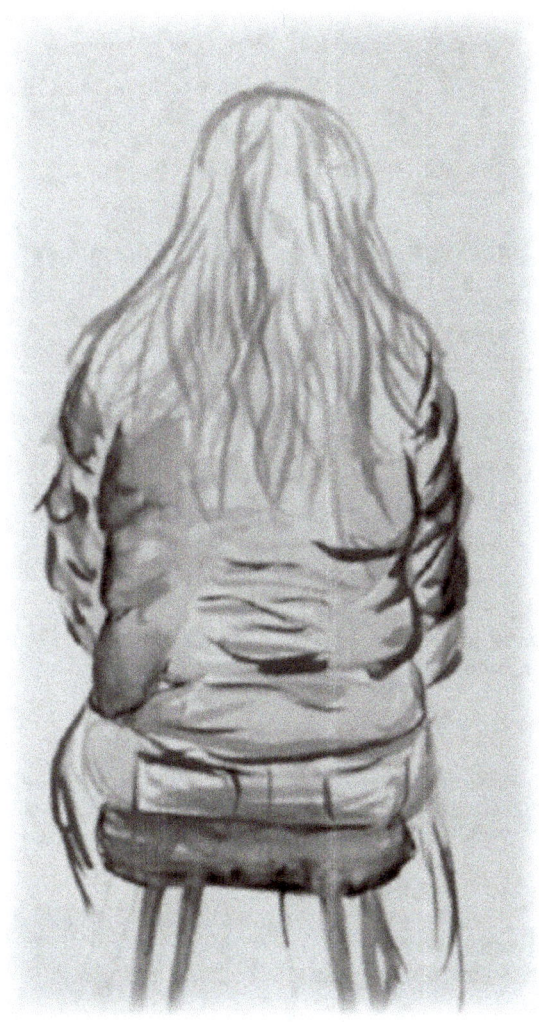

TWENTY

No one wants to see men who live without belief:
We want to see men who give life for His cause:
Not men who give life because He has none:
god knows its entertaining to see men die:
Blind and zealous.

The party leaders made blind zealots for show:
Educating children for...
Entertainment.
Unbeknownst to man:
The knowledge of good and evil lied with the
snake:
Character formed from Our following action.

He was no less god than you or me:
An old god acting an old man with one flaw:
man.

His age saw character:
Our character, which He made Us with the
knowledge of absolute good and absolute evil:
And an absolute understanding of Our good and
evil.
He saw.

The snake was named Lycane, because He was:
He gifted the knowledge of good and evil:
And from that was the protagonist born.

The viewers loved power.
They loved forcing ignorant men to fight without
their knowledge:
Of what everything was:

For what else made them gods?

The viewers loved power.
They loved forcing ignorant party leaders to
entertain them:
For what else made them gods:
But viewers?

The viewers wanted power:
Impossible in a free world.
They wanted excitement safe from harm:
Impossible in a free world.
Which is why slaves went to heaven:
And pretenders had less chance at Hell.
It was giving control:
Where the only choices:
Were no choices:
And given the choice between His world and ours...

He who made sin was bored:
While He who enjoyed uncontrollable sin was:
man.
Not dead:
But sleeping.
By the protagonist woken:
To sleep evermore.

While awake, men chanced on an interesting
conundrum:
That every man chanced on.
He was happiest knowing His place in the world:
And living moment by moment:
As opposed to living in the moment.
Although lies saw Him Hell:
Hell was just a moment of lies:
So He was happy:
In Hell.

Our happiness had strangeness about it:

That man was dishonestly satisfied with His honest dissatisfaction.
His lie was that everyone was happy:
Because no one was more happy:
Than He.
Haha.

What is man, if He is in Hell?
What is Hell, if man is in it?

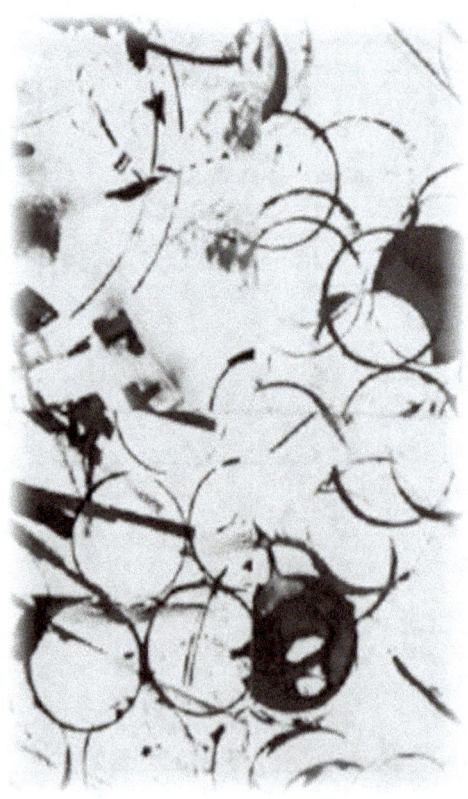

TWENTY-ONE

That was Her life's meaning, less the meaning and
more the,
Understanding.
A poor substitute:
Although she saw her house crumbling:
That didn't stop it falling down.

What could was man, who couldn't stop:
His vice:
And We the grateful slaves suffered.

He bent the brittle into the broken:
Who shattered from their laughing Death.
Blinded:
They returned to Him:
Their house of sand swept to the sea:
Of living lost dreams We were never meant to
have...

Houses were Our place of living:
Not a place of passing life:
But opportunity loved:
And opportunity lost.

My little girl's opportunity won, I gifted her
Death:
And released to the sea.

I wasn't god:
But as cancer consumed her:
I was all she believed in.
What else made Us gods?

Eric Spoerl

Her hair fell out.
It never grew back.
You want to know something funny?
Something awful?
That was the worst part.
When she opened her eyes:
Little girls reminded her what the world lost:
Or never had.

She hated them.

It was never about the hair.

She couldn't remember her hair color:
She didn't want to.

It was never about the hair.

She envied ignorance:
She saw:
A world beyond four walls:
Beyond human understanding:
Of meager survival:
So desperately far away.
Life was not meant without respite:
Life was not meant for her:
Our god.

She understood.
Man had been strangled by His lifeline:
Since the beginning of time.

She didn't hate man for freedom He didn't have:
His bliss meant nothing to her.

It was never about the hair.

She hated man's blindness to freedom.
Hanged by His noose:

88

In His lonely house:
Shackled to a lonely shore.

My little girl saw what man would be if He
realized His:
Cancer.
But blind men knew nothing.
Blind to His four walls:
Building until there was nothing to see.

She lied on His beach, gasping at the sight of
freedom:
If she could have run to it!
Unable to describe color to blind men:
A broken mute saw His revelation and cried.
If He would tear down His house He would see:
He would have to see!
Before man became crooked living lost dreams We
were never meant to have...

But He laughed at her.
As she saw His new horizon:
He saw nothing but His closest shore:
And she screamed:
If only He could see!

Blind men saw nothing:
Wanted to see nothing.

She hated His blank eyes under a perfect crop of
hair:
Only Cain left crop circles.

And god laughed at her lying on His beach:
Life was not meant without respite:
Life was not meant for her:
Trying to shepherd passive slaves nodding:
And on and on...

Eric Spoerl

Screaming freedom to blind men as they whiled
away:
Our existence,
And god laughed.

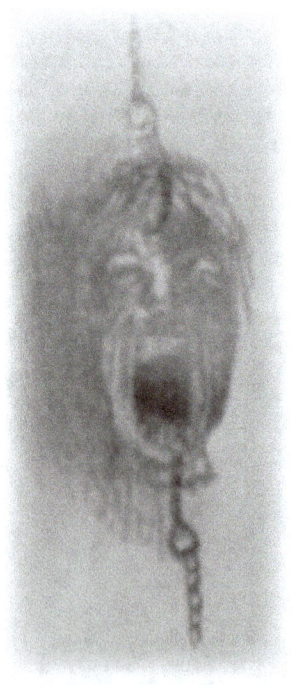

TWENTY-TWO

Educate:
A kaleidoscope of amorphous uniform colors:
And nameless.
After His noxious flame goes out:
It will do.

It should horrify Us:
Destroy Our faith in purpose:
While evolution breeds losers:
To live on.
If it doesn't make you sick enough to die, you're
not a monster:
Like me.

What is Our future:
But to be less like god than We ever were?
Sociopath's don't walk while dead:
And god doesn't lie sleeping:
He smolders:
Even after His flame's gone out.

The gods needed to burn:
So they made the antithesis of want:
The antagonist.
A man who did not want for himself:
But what was best for you and me:
While We watched His show:
And clapped.

Abraham educated an undeserving hatred:
And the gods applauded:
His hatred for:
Everything.

Eric Spoerl

He opposed the protagonist, and in the end:
Neither walked alive:
Or dead.
The antagonist set himself on fire:
To set the world aflame:
And watch it burn into blackened rock:
While His Hell did the same.
Was there a better reason?

Men believed they should die for their
protagonist and antagonist.
Not as obligation:
But privilege:
To die for their story.

The antagonist's men believed everything burned:
Especially freedom.
Blind men believed everything was worth burning:
For freedom.

And there was never a war between men, who were
corrupted:
Only infallible ideas.

Men who wanted to burn the world worse than the
world had burned them.
god wanted to burn the world:
For fun.

The party leaders needed me burned alive:
A charred corpse which no flood would lie:
With.
Someone to hate like god:
Someone to hate like man.

I was the first antagonist:
Killed as We all were:
By the wrath of Our benevolent Father.
Who did not distinguish between friend and foe,

for what was He but:
A man who had neither?

He looked down upon the righteous and the damned
and decided.
He looked down upon the men who would fight for
Him unto their last dying breath and decided.
He looked down upon the men who would fight
against Him unto their last dying breath and
decided.
He looked down upon dead men walking and
decided:
Burn them, He told Gabriel.
Gabriel asked how many.
All of them.
Adding Gabriel to the flames, god told himself:
This pleases me.
Was there a better reason?

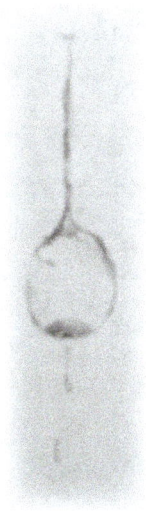

TWENTY-THREE

There was no sanity but the fortune of ignorance:
All men went insane eventually:
It was a question of when:
And the more time they had,...
Let Us pray.

She with the cracked god was about to crack from
Our:
Radiation.
Everything she knew:
Were her lies, not mine.

How long could she stare at His horizon?
How long could she scream color at blind men with
deaf ears?
Before she saw herself on that sandy shore:
A blind deaf man:
Content.

How long could We praise Our roof, blind to the
walls:
Wasting away with sand in Our eyes:
Living lost dreams We were never meant to have....

How long before you hated them for:
What they weren't:
And could never let you be.
Lying in sand, cold, naked and alone:
While they screamed meaningless platitudes...

She cracked.
And my sympathy was for naught when she:
Felt nothing.

Antagonist

You want to know something funny?
Something awful?
She didn't hate the bully:
She hated the spectators.

Her end is Ours.
Man is limited in suffering:
And god is bored.
Good things are good because they end:
Happily ever dead soon after.
Bad things are bad because they begin:
Once upon an endless time...
Ask Abraham.

Dying, my little girl saw the men who cried for
her and asked:

Why do you cry when your fears and tears are a lie:
You suffer, in your house of sand you say snuff
her:
Beached, broken and bullied by those who didn't
reach:
god's laugh, as He smashes sand you labored to
craft:
And I pray, not your fault god, not your fault, I
say:
But you. And you. And you. And you. And you. And
you.

She had a choice.
Prolong Her inevitable contingency plan:
Or:
Refuse treatment and die.
Exit Our game forever:
Just as she began.

You want to know something funny?
Something awful?
In real life, decisions look less like:

Eric Spoerl

Choices, choices, choices.
And more like:
Choice.

She spent her life struggling to breathe and
wracked with pain on successful effort:
Unable to let go.
Seeing something lost and forgotten; hopeful when
Death was the only escape and escape was the only
option.

I stayed with her unto the end:
Lying with my little girl as her teacher.
You want to know something funny?
Something awful?
No one suspected me.

I didn't leave when her dreams cracked from:
Everything:
She saw dull misgivings, the questions and
answers of a dead god on her mind:
A god man had forgotten, but she was burdened to
remember.
On Death's doorstep, she saw:
Everything.

Every moment the dying wake in pain and bitter
refusal to let go:
Although it's all they ever wanted:
And every moment they let go of letting go:
They see the world in a new light:
And on and on...
Praying their teacher would stop:
Stop! Stop!
In the end, they see what He wanted them to see:
In the beginning.
Education! Education! Not torture, but education!

Her Death was a vision of clarity:

She saw what I had done:
To everyone.

Who are you?
To god she whispered:

Nobody.

By the hand, that which rocked Our cradle:
He turned it over:
And upright again.

TWENTY-FOUR

Can you feel man laughing:
Maniacally, as only He can?
I don't care:
Nobody does.

Who are you?
Nobody.

You want to know something funny?
Something awful?
That defines the main character:
And the statistic:
Crying at the top of their lungs:
This is wrong! man is generous with His content:
This is wrong! man is greedy with His discontent.
I don't care:
Nobody does.

Who are you?
Nobody.

The antagonist matters most of all...
A man who does not want for himself:
But what is best for you and me:
While We watch His show:
And clap.

Without Him, We would collapse:
Under suffocating boredom.

Good thing We're human:
The universe needs a good antagonist:
A man who does not want for himself:

But what is best for you and me.

The universe needs life:
Who justifies the means.

I was the antagonist:
Opposed to perfection in all its imperfection:
Sam.
My protagonist:
As I was Our inspiration:
When We lost Our name for it:
We saw that:
We never knew.

Men worshipped Sam:
Who promised freedom from slavery:
Impossible in a free world.
It didn't exist:
The moment man felt most free:
Was the moment He was most enslaved:
By His choices, choices, choices:
Choice.

The saint died sleeping and evolution walked...

Men worshipped me for belonging:
Emaciated by men who saw them as:
Dead.
Broken until their pieces were unspeakably
monstrous:
Tormented into a senseless oblivion:
Oblivious to everything but anger:
Cutting those who picked them up:
Until no one tried.
And on and on...

Men worshipped me because they weren't dead:
But someone told them:
They were.

Eric Spoerl

They hated Us:
And god's hand didn't protect:
Anyone.
Us or them:
Although they hated Us:
We didn't know:
Who they were?

To win, We became:
Different.
Monstrous and godlike:
Entirely human.
What do the ends justify if not the means?

If a pig buys pork and eats it to become pork:
Who is more human?
For what do the ends justify if not the means?

TWENTY-FIVE

Murder kill and slaughter, He lured Us in with
laughter:
Nothing:
But strange fantasy and indifferent ecstasy, what
might entertain god that isn't
godly?

The girl who died at peace with the world:
Did not entertain:
No matter her purpose.
The girl who died with pride:
Who lied:
Did nothing for her master:
Although she was led into violent pastures:
She strayed to lie in a better place.

He needed broken:
Sharp.
Shattered, feeble, naked and wanting:
Without satisfaction:
Or perceivable hunger:
Just want.
His want.

gods wanted what they wanted when they wanted it:
Now.
Because wanting felt good:
And nothing else did.
They needed it:
Eternally:
Sinful...

For it gods wait:

And on and on...
As far from god as you or me:
Leaving them waiting for:
Ever.

All men go insane eventually:
It is a question of when.
Good things are good because they end:
Happily ever dead soon after.
Bad things are bad because they begin:
Once upon an endless time...

god needed:
To see how insecure security was:
And breathe however possibly:
Short.
Choices, choices, choices:
Choice.
Our destruction is freedom?
His destruction is Hell.

It was plot and conclusion:
Characters He gasped after drowning under
boredom:
Pacing Our world with:
His wants.

god needed:
Puppets:
Men without feeling:
Lying under:
His wants.
Not Ours.

My purpose was not His:
My entertainment not for:
Anyone.
It didn't matter that I loved her:
It never did.

Antagonist

I saw it:
And couldn't stop.

In the eyes of every girl I murdered for blind
purpose:
I saw what Katie saw:
Never before and never again.

The truth was:
Beautiful.
What do the ends justify if not the means?

I saw it in my little girl:
Murdered for His:
Purpose.

It was plot and conclusion:
Choices, choices, choices:
Choice.
She screamed kill me!
Blind men collapsed under her weight:
But no one could empathize with her sympathy:
She killed them for trying.
I think she cried, but her tears mixed with the
water so it was hard for anyone to tell:
Least of all, me.
Least of everything, me.

Who are you?
Nobody.

She was beautiful.
I didn't kill my little girl:
She did.
She opened her eyes:
And couldn't unlearn what she had learned.

She saw Our cancer:
For what else made her god?

Eric Spoerl

We laughed at the Hell We made:
And as We toasted the gods of emaciation, someone shouted:
Life, liberty, and the pursuit of happiness!
We cheered hooray!

god cried himself to sleep that night:
And after my drink:
I did too.

TWENTY-SIX

gods:
As proponents of liberty, they were proponents of
a false liberty:
As men fallen from Earth:
Into unimaginable Hell...

We were welcomed there:
And left to die:
While I hungered:
For their wants.

Heroes don't dismember children:
Without crying.
But disembodied children wonder:
What does it matter?

After blood falls:
And gore paints the heavens and the Earth:
What does it matter:
If We were only human?

Abraham left me dying:
Stranded on a beach without sand:
Suffocating under waves without shelter:
I think I cried, but my tears mixed with the water
so it was hard for anyone to tell:
Least of all, me.
Least of everything, me.

dogs nibbled at Our heels while We slept:
And laughed when We woke smothered by what We
deemed unimportant:
Without limbs to push it off.

Eric Spoerl

The vicious dogged the noble:
Because it entertained:
But whatever purpose:
You were dead:
Even if you were the dog.

If absolute power corrupted absolutely:
What did absolute lack of power do?
For what else made Him god?

As brothers fought over field and flock:
The knowledge of good and evil forgot:
My Father taught me to tread:
And the snake taught Sam to:
Slither.
They did not make men:
For there was never a war between men, who were
corrupted:
Only infallible ideas.

I was an emotionally barren man, who succeeded
not because I was without scruples and willing
to kill, but because I was without scruples and
wanting to kill:
I painted the heavens and the Earth with gore:
Unflinchingly entertaining.

I wasn't His follower:
Wasn't His friend:
For what was a god but a man who had neither?

He was my Father:
Old through virtuous character:
Or lack of both.
In Hell:
We saw Death:
But didn't understand:
Why We were emaciated.
Haha.

He killed men who lost sight of something:
We couldn't know.
Our perception was:
Wrong.
It was fair:
What else was Hell?

Before ripping blind men limb from limb, He
seized them by the throat and smashed their head
into the wall, letting them crumple to the floor.
Lying to men in a pool of blood, He would lean in
and whisper:
Who are you?

As my emaciation grew:
So my education grew to a close.
Before ripping me limb from limb, He seized me
by the throat and smashed my head into the wall,
letting me crumple to the floor.
Lying to man in a pool of blood, He leaned in and
whispered:
Who are you?
To my god I whispered:

Nobody.

Abraham's lips curled upwards in a way that
curdled milk.
A shudder emanated through the room:
Along with several suicides.
He told me starving sheep made:
Wolves.

I was a wolf born into absolutism:
The only man there ever was.
Grateful:
To have a purpose.
Entertaining:
With the fire of Our Hell because:

Eric Spoerl

Everything burned.

TWENTY-SEVEN

The dead cannot experience Hell:
Alive We See:
And dead lie:
Dreaming.

His giving took:
Everything.
He taught man to tread:
Into Hell:
Where He knew of freedom:
But couldn't dream without:
Dying.

You want to know something funny?
Something awful?
In real life, monsters make:
Choices, choices, choices.
Men make:
Choice.

We chose suicidal hatred:
Lying under His suffocating:
Choices.

Do you know how to catch a monster?
Men don't like to talk about it:
But there is only one way.

Once drowning, men understand:
Their house was always:
Made of sand.

The dead cannot experience Hell:

Eric Spoerl

Alive We see:
And dead lie:
Dreaming.

That was the joke.
Monsters saw what could have been:
Before what would always be.
There was no monster:
Like perspective.

Our sacrifice was spat on:
I think We cried, but Our tears mixed with the
water so it was hard for anyone to tell:
Least of all, me.
Least of everything, me.

god laughed and I shuddered.

Let Us pray:

A fox in a foxhole, We're all there, We pay toll:
Eager to enervate, gather stores so meager:
For an inspired hole, out of mud, not quagmire:
Some pups survive, a success merely to derive:
Life might not be awful; god gives Us a paw-full:
An untimely doom, your pelt shall furnish His
room.

TWENTY-EIGHT

I despise tradition:
And Our tradition of entertainment, however
glorious:
If there was glory in Our suicidal tradition:
Of entertainment.

Ridiculous to carry:
And cast aside.
We wanted to walk unburdened:
But needed tradition:
For the glory of:
Entertainment.

My Father made me:
And His Father before Him:
And on and on...
Abraham made me:
To kill for tradition:
And let He who suffered at my hands condemn.
Blind men:
Wanted my Death like drowning men want air:
Gasping under domestic limbs and it was:
Glorious.
But what was Our:
Choice?

I lost my perception:
Under a roof with no walls:
I saw everywhere but:
Up.
I lost my home:
And everything since was:
Looking.

Wondering:
Who was more human?
Who died from Our:
Insanity?

Was it the little girl:
Hanged for her blanket:
When He had too many?
Who died?
Was it the little boy:
Who hanged her for air:
Closing His eyes to her perception:
Who died?
In Our world of:
Choice.

You want to know something funny?
Something awful?
I was an emotionally barren man, who succeeded
not because I was without scruples and willing
to kill, but because I was without scruples and
wanting to kill.

We didn't fear men who killed out of desperation:
Because desperate men had reasons to be:
Desperate...
And no matter Our drowning:
Pretending to survive was:
Surviving.

Do you know how to catch a monster?
Men don't like to talk about it:
But there is only one way.

I strangled her:
Took her intestines and made a noose for her to
swing with.
Remaking my perception:
Rejecting the world We made.

Antagonist

The frightened closed their eyes:
Knowing without:
Understanding.
I was cavernous and monstrous, choking on Our
worldly:
Sight:
Of a little girl hanged by her intestines, crying:
Education! Education! Not torture, but education!
My emaciation...
Some fought:
And some crawled to Our unnatural beast sprawled
across His Earth to bow and whisper:
Praise.

He broke them, torn apart limb from limb.
When the men were meat He devoured them, sparing
the sight they were never more.
Everything burned.
Was there a better reason?

Who are you?
Nobody.

TWENTY-NINE

We didn't want:
Us or them.
Although they Hated Us:
We didn't know:
Who they were?

We needed:
Us or them.
My power was as baseless:
As baseless men.
Nothing, but perceivably everything:
From man's emaciation and woman's:
Burning.
To Us, then:
Everyone.

Although infallible idea's never died:
men did.

Power destroyed men:
Blinding Us to Our perceptive:
Drowning.
Power made gods:
And destroyed them too.

men went insane.
Some craved women:
Some depraved women:
They drowned in madness from the drought.
Some hated me for removing their strength:
Some hated me for removing their weakness:
Abraham asked who tilled the fields:
And herded the sheep?

What did I become to destroy a monster:
What did a monster become to survive?
The birth of power birthed a monster:
And the Death of power was Ours too:
So while Sam led blind men:
I destroyed what they had.

THIRTY

He took Our love first:
god knows why.
Sad man's laughter was:
Hollow.
And He emaciated.

His laughter was:
Tragedy that tempted:
Without necessity:
But want.

It was not what tragedy did to man:
But man to himself:
That was appealing.

What is Hell, but Earth when compared to heaven?
A perfect construct of Our imperfect mind.

The dead cannot experience Hell:
Alive We see:
And dead lie:
Dreaming.

THIRTY-ONE

It was a dream wove of vapor, perceptively
substantial rather than:
Lucid, We were never lucid:
Anymore...
I tread the road through Our wilderness, screams
ringing like echoes underwater:
The snuffling whimpers of winners losing:
Alone, beasts without language or:
Comfort.

Has there ever been a monster with friends?
He is cruel circumstance:
Giving nothing:
For He has less.
To do so would have been tragic:
For man didn't have the friends:
To die.

The wounded children saw sympathy dying:
If only they had the empathy to do themselves the
same...
They were in Hell:
Afraid to die.

The dead cannot experience Hell:
Alive We see:
And dead lie:
Dreaming.

I have nightmares about the acrid smell:
Bloody, distinct, metallic flavor:
Searing the noses of men left to rot:
Since birth.

When do children grown up?
When they don't vomit while wading through
corpses:
Or when they see nothing:
In a world unchanged.

Blind men guarded Our burning sanctity:
Hidden deep in their wilderness.
Past the soldiers of blind revolution:
The only kind there ever was.

I gutted them.

Treading through their wilderness, I lied where
blind men couldn't see:
Under darkness smothering the unimportant.
I gutted them:
The guards of a treasure:
Burning out.

Out.
I extinguished the flames one by one:
Ending a drought:
By the women who caused it.
Shhhhh.
Go to sleep...

Who are you?
Nobody.

***

Hate is unlike fickle man:
A perfect construct of Our imperfect mind:
Godlike, but entirely:
Human.

It implies necessary compulsion:
Destruction despite the damage.

Antagonist

The inhuman absolutism:
Of a human mind.
A needless purpose:
Gifted by the antagonist:
To the necessary protagonist:
And on and on...

Blind men were gifted hate with purpose:
The only kind there ever was.
A new Hell...

For there was never a war between men, who were
corrupted:
Only infallible ideas.

With man's blood the price to pay:
We made war with hatred:
And although We knew what We had to do, We didn't
understand.

Blind men could feel:
But couldn't care:
Lying in the notion they had nothing to lose.
A joke.

Sam deprived men of cheap human meaning:
On the theory that nothing, had meaning at all.

I gifted Sam the knowledge of good and evil:
And after Sam indulged:
Who was more human:
In Our emaciation.

Do you know how to catch a monster?
What a hero would have to do...
What We had to become.
To misunderstand and maneuver such unrestrained
insanity was:
Nothing short of absolution.

Eric Spoerl

Do you know how to catch a monster?
Win.

THIRTY-TWO

My Father educated:
Choice.
Monkey see, monkey do:
Children gods are monkeys too.

But old gods never choose truth:
Over what they know is true.
Monkey see, monkey won't:
Understand.

If pleading indifference pleased Him:
Monkey see, monkey do.
We forgot what We knew:
Children gods are monsters too.

man was the end all be all:
And We would end it:
Without knowing Us faulty:
Or faultless.
So We saw both:
And gods saw a perception:
That didn't exist.

Not right and wrong:
But mine and not mine.
god saw the pattern:
His brother another.
And on and on...

We see beginning and ending:
Uncomprehending.
gods that We are:
Monster see, monster do.

Choices, choices, choices:
Choice.
We see Our perception changing:
Nothing.

Because blind men with deaf ears:
Don't have the empathy to do themselves the same...
Monkey see, monster do.

THIRTY-THREE

What if weren't meant to fear monsters:
But didn't have the empathy to do Ourselves the
same?
What We needed:
To be winners.

Making cannon fodder without entertainment:
Least of all Our own.
It's a wonder We don't squirm:
Like pigs eating pork.

Inhuman monsters and gods:
Who said We were human?

They called me the Devil:
A monster:
Not me, not me.

The Devil was a winner:
god named Him monster:
But how do We know:
Which is which?

We condemn casting the first stone:
And celebrate the last.
What god would have to become:
To kill a monster, if there was anything but:
god.
Who was more human:
In His emaciation?

Every hero is god:
When We lose:

Eric Spoerl

We tell the story of a Devil:
In His emaciation.

I was a prophet of freedom:
No one knew:
Until they lost more.

Free will was His tragedy:
Worshipping man for no better reason than being:
man.

We drowned the Devil:
And His blood-bloated corpse has:
Rotten:
Like every other god.

Lying in Our cesspool We held His head under:
And saw there is no you and me, only:
Us.
Rotten:
Like every other god.

He laughed when We saw what was real and what was
actually:
Beautiful.
No monsters, no gods, only:
man.

THIRTY-FOUR

The pain We suffer does not mean man lacks
wanting:
But that He wants.
The humanity We suffer does not mean man lacks
wanting:
But that He wants.

Godliness is the gift of man:
The sympathy of unresolved absolutism:
Without the empathy to understand:
The knowledge of good and evil:
Was never there.

Man is a puppet:
To every authority but His own:
As He pulls Our strings:
Blind to His own:
Who are you?
Nobody.

Unable to understand Our burning absolutism:
Slaves saw what they needed:
All along.

Despite the ash, He endured:
The story He was reduced to.
That living was better than living as:
man.
A:
Slave.
Slowly:
Dying.

Eric Spoerl

Monkey see, monkey do:
Without clay in a world of ash.

Pain was painful for man's want of:
Living.

I didn't cry for the men who would die:
I cried for the men who would live.

THIRTY-FIVE

The world crumbled:
Eventually.
With the motives that left it dying:
The gods gasped in need of ending:
If only they had the empathy to do themselves the
same...

Abraham left.
It didn't matter:
We all did.

Our bodies sacrificed to the show:
Our choice.
In broken, emaciated:
Freedom.

My Father left Our war between infallible ideas:
A corrupted slave to Our:
Absolutism:
The only kind there ever was.

Who are you?
Nobody.

We made a world where:
Winners died and losers fled:
Emaciated.
Our enemies, Our friends:
Were men of cruel circumstance.

They were my sheep and I their shepherd:
In this awful world We made:
Who understood but couldn't:

Know that sight wasn't:
Enough.

Men wanted freedom:
But needed:
To praise their god and march in time.

Sam revolutionized:
Our equal inequality.
Unhappy with cruel circumstance, We needed Our:
Emaciation:
In Our world of men:
Sam believed in man:
And choices, choices, choices:
When We needed, Our:
Choice.

Blind men tried to gouge out Our eyes:
Surrounding Us on the mountaintop:
Crying:
If only I spilled enough red:
I might see.

They saw slavery:
But couldn't understand:
man was chained in His cave:
Seeing shadows and screaming:
This is everything!

Not knowing how to see:
They ignored Him:
Screaming softly.

Trying to choose:
They were blind to Our:
Choice.

They cut the blanket in half for two shivering
emaciated men and left them to die for no better

reason than because they were:
Emaciated.
Making fairness:
And Our cruel circumstance, although dog ate dog:
man did far worse:
With the knowledge of good and evil.

We chose to do:
Anything to anyone:
Anywhere.

We stole the blanket from two shivering emaciated
men for no better reason than because they were:
Emaciated...

Was there a better reason?

THIRTY-SIX

Left lying in the cave a dead man sleeping:
To wake up and walk in three days time...
It was too cold.
We burned Our blankets, a:
Choice?
We were killing and dying:
But men always died.
Then the food stopped.

On Our side there was a pipe from which all water
flowed:
We could take the water or let it drain:
But the water was always flowing.
It was yellow and brackish from cycling through:
But what more could We want?

On their side there was a pipe from which all food
flowed:
They could take the food or let it drain:
But the food was always flowing.
It was rotten meat and moldy bread:
But what more could they want?

Who are you?
Nobody.

Every day We exchanged water for food:
Until We didn't.
It stopped.

We made a war We could see but couldn't:
Understand.
We lost in Our:

Antagonist

Emaciation.

I couldn't understand such absolutism:
Nobody could.
Nobody could have understood Our crawling to:
Resolution.

Our fight had evolved into something more
monstrous than We were capable of understanding:
But We tightened Our belts and marched into:
War:
Where winning:
Was losing and:
Who was more human?

We didn't talk to the other side:
We didn't try.

Absolutism was strangely lucid.

The men were so afraid:
I heard them crying, sometimes.
Their men were so afraid:
I heard them crying, sometimes.
I was so afraid.

We weren't ready for cruel circumstance:
Leaving Us nothing:
But Ourselves?

It wasn't because We were slaves:
It wasn't because We were human:
We were:
Hungry.
All the time.
But We almost forgot:
While feasting on their organs:
To the lullaby of:
War.

War over Our humanity:
And to the winner went the spoils.

Rats couldn't sate:
Our empathy.
We were alone:
And wanted nothing.
Our salvation:
Or nothing.

We burned Ourselves for wanting:
To burn them more:
Not win Our war.

Winning through attrition:
Was losing less.
And without their stockpile:
Our ribs were clawing out Our chests.

Choices, choices, choices:
Choice.
We had spent too much time with nothing to show
but swollen bellies and sunken eyes:
What We had to become...

men blind to their stockpile:
Didn't know it wasn't enough:
When We had nothing:
They weren't men.

Emaciated soldiers killing for no better reason
than because the others were:
Emaciated.
What those pigs did for pork.

I knew Sam was real:
Had to be real:
Not actually:
Beautiful.

Our soldiers collapsed, from lack of water and
food.
Bellies distilled and bursting, piss black from
impurity:
Or crying from tortured bodies and vicious
looking bones:
With funny motivation.

Because even when We had enough food or water to
die, We were still:
Emaciated.

We crawled away:
Losers all:
Weak bodied, no one won:
What would that have been?
Eating rats and licking condensation:
For Our:
Choices, choices, choices:
Choice.

THIRTY-SEVEN

Desperation begot a desperate war:
The only kind there ever was.
Winners knew but couldn't:
Understand.
Our ends justified the means:
And We had Ourselves to blame.

We couldn't survive:
Even when We had enough food or water to die, We
were still:
Emaciated.

We didn't fight to win:
But to eat His flesh and drink His blood:
Because winning wasn't:
Entertaining.

I don't blame them for the war:
How can I?
We were so afraid.

But if the ends justify the means:
Then to no end:
They had no means:
And that is inhumane.

We were human.
Led like sheep unto Our shepherd:
Only because We were:
Human.
Led into fields of conflict:
For no better reason than because We were:
Emaciated.

Antagonist

Even when dying of malnutrition:
Our family lying on the ground:
Pathetic lumps of sick and Death:
We tightened Our belts and marched on:
Once more into the breach.
Better than monsters:
We were men!
gods of a dissimilar fate:
For god never wore a belt so tight:
Or slept with maggots and cannibals:
He walked with them:
Forever.

THIRTY-EIGHT

I was my Father's price for a peaceful life:
Nothing personal.
Just money.

Orphaned to cruel circumstance:
By parents of blood:
Not choice.

A burden.
That's what He called me.

When I hit myself with His old leather belt:
He smiled:
I did too.

On Our mountaintop He gifted me to god:
As His Father before Him:
And on and on...

My brother lied in the fields He tilled:
My mother was:
Nothing.

I was payment for the life He wasted:
His suffering equal to:
Everyone else's:
And mine equal to His:
When He offered me as His price to be paid.

I was equal to all children:
As they were equal to me.
Upon birth in His house of sand:
We were thrown face-first into the sea.

I couldn't understand His:
Perception:
At the whim of Our bored god:
They offered my entertainment:
For themselves.

It was July 8th some misbegotten year:
And I was hungry.
Katie left:
And I set myself on fire:
To burn the world worse than I had been burned.

It was easy:
They used sleeping pills for their:
Emaciation.
All I did was watch the house burn.

They screamed before men came:
To watch like me.
And it was actually:
Beautiful.

Who are you?
Nobody.

I didn't hate them for what they pretended to be:
I was a:
god.
Their ends justified my means.
Who lost:
But the man in the sky who had:
Nothing?
I smiled.

THIRTY-NINE

man was still: Hungry.
man was still: Thirsty.
Though We lived in the Garden of Eden:
Whose garden was it?

man had gone from frightened to frightening:
He hadn't eaten in:
Far.
Too.
Long.
He became monstrous:
His bones too poignant:
And His flesh was...
Stretched.
Sulking on bones like excess weakness:
His muscles starved.
Emaciated before He was dead:
Dead before He stopped walking.
His eyes saw honest hate:
I had caused His suffering:
And there was no payment:
For peace.
It didn't matter why, all that mattered was god
made man:
Emaciated.

We only understood what We had lost:
And if I could have destroyed everything in a slow
instant, I would have done it:
No matter how slow:
No matter how gruesome, if it was done:
It would have been less agonizing than that
moment:

Antagonist

One honest moment, where I should have told them
We lost.

What Sam and I did was not honest:
And I would have killed them to be rid of their
accusing eyes...

We didn't want survival:
We wanted ending;
If only We had the empathy to do Ourselves the
same.
I couldn't help them:
So I told them We could win:
Once more into the breach.

I used cannon fodder for entertainment:
Catching blind men unaware.
No one was aware, anymore:
Look at Us,
Little children beating littler children to
Death:
What were We but:
Cannon fodder?

There was a terrific crash when Our armies met:
And childish hands did childish work:
And the screaming...
As one side drowned the other:
Little hands pushed little heads under:
For the first time We:
Saw.

I saw Sam.

Imagine this:
When I thought about Sam, the sum of all matters
great and small were:
Nothing.
I loathed myself more for every moment I spent on

139

other thoughts:
Until Sam consumed me.
When I was near Sam, I was happier dying than
leaving:
While away, I couldn't die without seeing Sam one
last time.
No matter what Sam asked me to do, I would have
done it:
To myself, to anybody:
I suppose I did.
Haha.

I felt a stabbing pain:
And as I fell, Sam's crude rock tearing holes in my
chest:
I screamed:
I've given you everything!
My men converged to consume the corpse that was
Sam:
And, blood spurting out of my chest with every
gasping heave, I began to laugh uncontrollably:
As I fell from the chasm of my life, into a void
more piercing than the eyes of my love, I found I
couldn't' remember why I was falling:
Falling.
Haha.

FORTY

Waves of color and sound unimaginable and
unperceivable attacked my eyes and ripped
through the fabric of my thought:
I was dying.

I looked at myself and saw:
A kaleidoscope of amorphous uniform colors.
I was:
Nameless.

Although I was floating through space, lifted
upwards, ever upwards with each passing moment
I felt surer to be falling closer to the doom
awaiting me:
Peacefully.

It was not a concept, but a stray notion clung to
like a child to His mother:
A notion that had to come from the colors I
couldn't see and the sounds I couldn't hear, for
although I had fought it my whole life, I was blind
and deaf.
That notion wove and re-wove the fabric of my
being so many times I threatened to lose myself
entirely:
I might have lost myself entirely.

Each human construct had new ideas, concepts and
notions itself, inconsistent and unmemorable,
except for:
Fear.

Eric Spoerl

Permeating through my perception, it was
something I once knew but had forgotten with each
passing moment:
And I was still floating:
Falling:
Upwards.
As I flew closer to whatever I was falling towards,
my fantasy became more and more ridiculous and
conceited, vague and frightening.
Less and less human with every thought and...

The emotions sweeping through me like the tides
of countless planets were not the monstrosity of
man.

Each notion was more meaningful and meaningless
as I pushed aside everything that had meaning.
I didn't' know what to think:
Not that it mattered.

As I accelerated upwards, falling through the sky,
my perception became more overwhelming and the
emotions sweeping away my constructs grew more
absolute and strange:
Something destroyed my undesirable parts and
replacing them with itself, so pleasing.

As I hurtled into the distance I was crying and
crying:
All the way home!
All the way home.

FORTY-ONE

It stopped.
You want to know something funny?
Something awful?
I wonder,

god and His:
Notions, appeared before me.

He wouldn't let me go.
I was furious.

I wasn't His anymore.
I had sanctified the mountaintop:
And laid Him to rest:
In the fires of Hell.

As I stared into god's face, I could have sworn He
looked sad.

Who are you?
To Our god I whispered:

Nobody.

REPORT: FILE #32

Case

of

Patient 26

Sam Samson M.D.

8, July

Patient 26 died today. We found him
in bed, hand chewed off and fingers
in his stomach. He finished his story
with Nobody and held it while he
died;

Without warning. It was his birthday.
His psychiatric report is thin; he
hasn't talked since his sister died;
His parents burned alive, although he
liked them dead, he thought;
They deserved it, for hurting Kratice until
she asked him for her;
Murder.
That much is clear.

We'd hoped he would write down
names and numbers, but the book is

opaque:
We speculate from here.

When his family died, no one would
adopt, so Patient 26 went to
home after home:
Became more alone:
And little girls died:
Always with brown hair, always with
brown eyess
Always the same age as him
and his sister:
Had she been alive.

We think he's killed two hundred
and five:
But we don't know how many he
changed:
Into something that'd rather have
died.

We worked so hard to have him:
And figure out his lie:
To make sense of his sickness:
Before it let him die:
We hope we'll get another:
So we can ask it why:

I know if our God loves us
Then he will help us try.

There will never be a man:
Like Lyane.
Haha.

S___ S_____, MD

By the hand, that which rocked
Our cradle.
He turned it over;
And upright again.

End

Eric Spoerl spent his childhood an outdoorsman, athlete and writer. His love for nature, (only rivaled by the books which cut it down), led him to become an Eagle Scout after 12 years of Scouting. During that time Eric relaxed by reading, often more than one book a day and writing what he found beautiful. Antagonist is his first novel.